THE
LIGHTNING BOLT

MICHAEL BEDARD
ILLUSTRATED BY REGOLO RICCI

TORONTO
OXFORD UNIVERSITY PRESS
1989

Oxford University Press, 70 Wynford Drive, Don Mills, Ontario, M3C 1J9

Toronto Oxford New York Delhi Bombay Calcutta Madras Karachi
Petaling Jaya Singapore Hong Kong Tokyo Nairobi Dar es Salaam
Cape Town Melbourne Auckland

and associated companies in
Berlin Ibadan

Canadian Cataloguing in Publication Data

Bedard, Michael, 1949–
The lightning bolt

ISBN 0-19-540732-6

I. Ricci, Regolo II. Title.

PS8553.E298L54 1989   jC813′.54   C89-090074-4
PR9199.3.B43Li 1989

Oxford is a trademark of Oxford University Press
1 2 3 4 — 2 1 0 9
Printed in Hong Kong

For Rebekah
— M.B.

To the memory of my father
— R.R.

It was just mid-morning, but you would never have known it by the look of the sky. With each passing moment it grew darker and darker still. Great black clouds blew in and clashed and rumbled against one another overhead, quite chasing the sun from the sky in fright. And the old woman gathering wood in the forest below was, if truth be told, a little frightened herself.

"How dark the day becomes," she thought. "Why, it's more like midnight than morning." And picking up what few sticks she had gathered, and throwing her axe over her shoulder, she hurried home as fast as her legs could carry her.

It wasn't much of a home at all, covered with bark and built of limbs fallen from trees and sticks from the forest floor. In fact, it so blended with the forest itself that a stranger passing there might have a hard time telling the house from the surrounding wood. As she walked through the door, her husband looked over at her from his seat before the fire.

"And what are you doing back so soon?" he snapped. "You haven't near enough wood to sell yet. And if you don't sell your wood, there'll be nothing left to eat and we'll both go hungry." And he shook his finger at her and stamped his foot on the floor.

He was not a pleasant old man in the least, and the older he got, the more ill-tempered he became, leaving the woman no peace at all. So she in fact looked forward to her time in the wood alone each day with something like delight.

"Storm's brewing," she said, sitting herself down by the window, which by now gave very little light, for it grew darker and more ominous by the minute.

"Nonsense," he said and wagged his finger at her once more.

Just then the sky seemed to split, and the forest was filled for an instant with light. A great jagged bolt of lightning shot down and with a deafening crash felled a gnarled old tree in the wood nearby. Then, just as suddenly as it had darkened, the sky grew light again.

By early afternoon the woman was off once more into the forest for her wood.

Well, the first thing she did was go directly to the smoldering old tree. It had been cut cleanly down the middle as though by some great axe wielded by a giant woodsman. The two halves of the tree had fallen to the forest floor on either side. You can scarcely imagine the old woman's surprise as she looked down at the base of the tree and saw there, in the centre of the trunk leading down into the ground below, a hole just large enough that a person might pass through. Coming from the hole was the most mournful moaning she had ever heard.

She stooped over and peered down into the dark, but could see nothing. So, summoning all her courage, she lowered herself down into the hole and stood silently in the dark amidst the moaning.

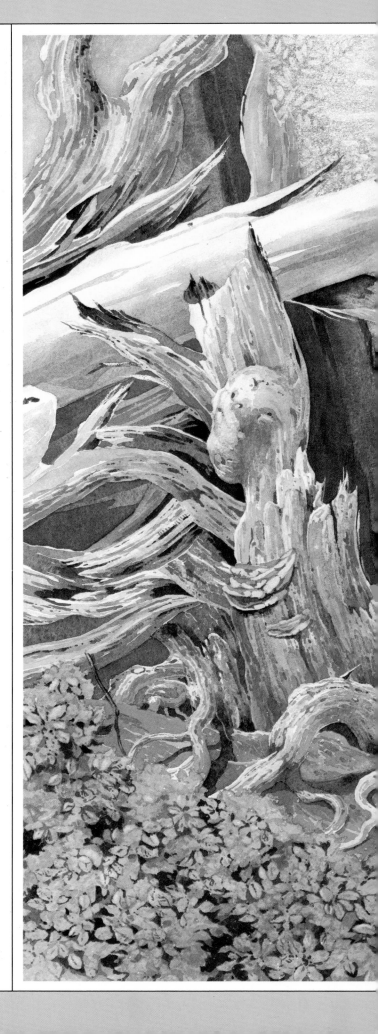

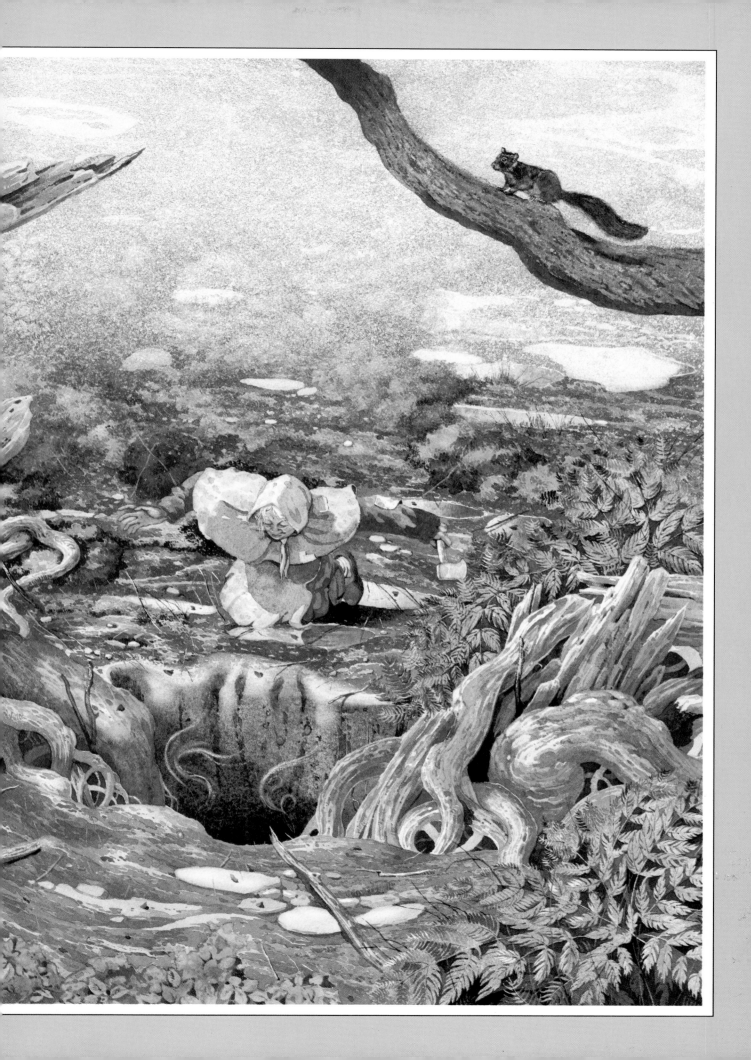

Gradually her eyes became accustomed to the blackness. She made out first the twisted roots of the tree all tangled this way and that and weaving downward into the earth.

Then gradually she made out among the roots the form of a queer little man. He was not much bigger than a boy, but he had a long grey beard that grew like moss entwined in the roots about him. And the beard was not the only thing twisted in the roots, for the little man himself was bound in by them. They wound about his arms and legs and wrapped about his body like some great snake so that he could not move at all and only moaned and groaned as he struggled in his bonds.

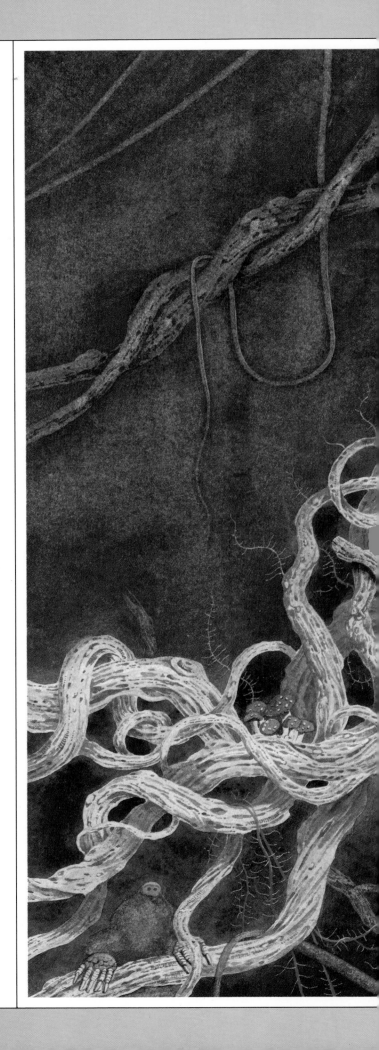

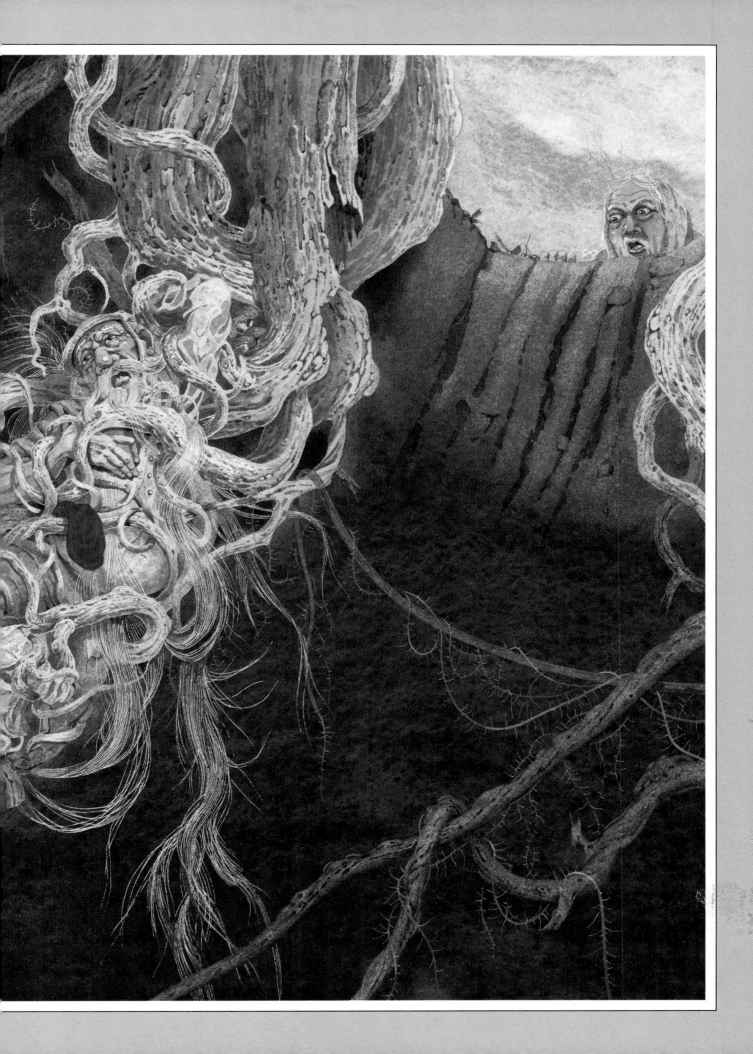

The old woman, with no more than half a thought, turned and pulled herself up through the hole, fetched her axe and dropped down again, where she immediately set to chopping at the roots. In a short time she had freed the little man and his great grey beard from their bonds. He jumped to his feet in joy, did a little dance and bounded up through the hole, with the old woman fast upon his heels.

"Thank you, friend," he said, making a deep bow and chuckling with delight. "I thought I might never get free of that terrible tree."

He was a crooked little man, as you might be had you been twisted and tangled in those roots as long as he. He carried in his hand a crooked stick that had lain by his side below. And he pulled from his pocket and put upon his head a crushed and tattered velvet cap.

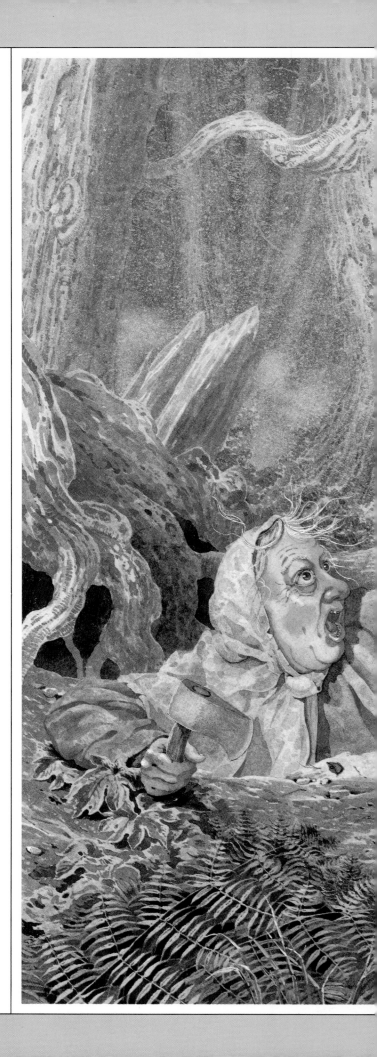

Turning to the old woman he said, "Well now, my good woman, you've done me a good turn and I must do you the same. Now, let me see. If truth be told, I've precious little to offer you. But here, take my stick and my cap. They might be of some good still—that is, if their magic hasn't moldered under there." And he kicked the tree with his foot.

"You need but wish with the stick, and what you wish will be. But the cap is best by far. Simply put it on your head and push it to one side, so, and you will see the secret thoughts of those you look upon as clearly as if they'd told you them themselves. Now, I can tell right off that you're a good sort and will use the gifts well. But if by chance you need me again, then make your way back here by dark of night, when thunder swells and lightning threads the sky, and I'll be here."

And so saying, he gave the old woman the stick and put the cap upon her head. Then he wound his great grey beard twice about his neck and was gone.

Off she went straight to her little shack, and there was her husband sitting by the fire as usual, and ill-tempered, which was equally as usual.

"Well, I see you've been hard at work again," he said, eyeing her narrowly and looking at the stick she carried. "How are we to put food on the table when all you bring home is one lone little stick like that? And where on earth did you get that ridiculous hat?"

The woman pushed the cap to one side and her mouth fell open, for his every thought spilled out before her as though he had told her himself. And if what he said was ill-humoured, what he thought was a hundred times worse. Why, she almost took up her stick and beat him with it. But she stopped herself in time and told him all that had passed with the little man and the tree. Well, almost all, for though she spoke of the stick's powers, she said nothing at all of the power of the cap. So for all he knew, it was simply a ridiculous looking crushed cap she had found along the way.

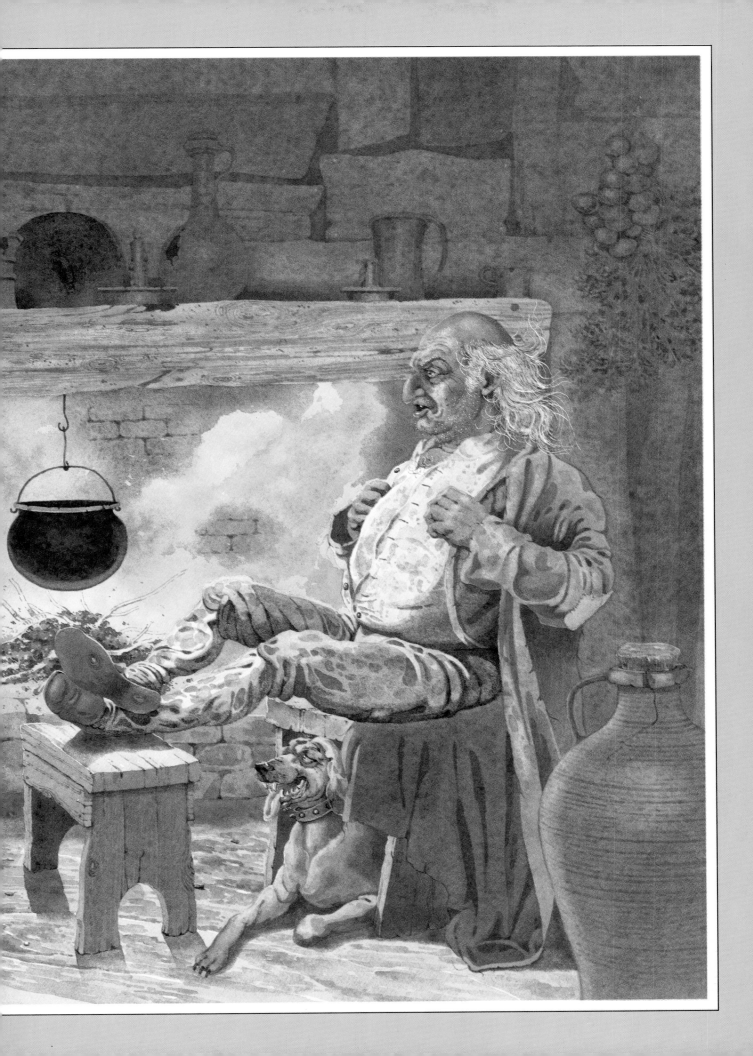

He snatched the stick from her hand and flung it into the fire. "I wish you'd get some dinner for me and leave off with your silly stories of little men in trees."

Now, no sooner had he said this than the table was filled to overflowing with fine food and strong drink such as neither of them had dreamt of before. The woman ran to the fire to rescue the stick. It had not so much as been blackened by the blaze.

"Well, what do you think of that?" said her husband.

And when they had recovered their senses they sat down to the most delicious meal they had ever tasted, the husband eyeing the stick by his wife's side all the while. When dinner was done, he snatched the stick from her and wished for a great brass bed with satin sheets to sleep in. So large was it that it quite filled up the shack. They went straight to bed and slept soundly until morning.

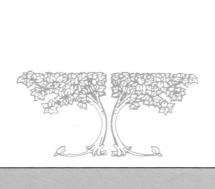

When the morning came it was immediately apparent that the bed was far too large for their little house. So the man wished for a great house, and he filled it with the finest furniture and he wished the finest clothes to fill the closets and for sacks of gold to be scattered everywhere. Before long he had to wish for a castle to contain all the things he had wished for as well as attendants to tend it and wait upon their wants.

In no time at all he had wished himself into a great king ruling over a vast realm, with all the wealth and power one could hope for. You might suppose that at last, then, he would be happy. But it was not so. The richer and more powerful he grew, the more cruel he became, especially towards his wife. So things with her went from bad to worse.

And whenever she put on her magic cap, she saw that he thought things a thousand times worse than what he said, and that was no comfort at all. At last one day she discovered that he had made up his mind to murder her and share the stick's magic with no one.

Frightened, she stole off with it and buried it beneath the castle wall. But it made such a frightful stir that the very walls began to shake and rumble and seemed ready to fall about her, so she took it out. Then she hid it in the closet, but it battered and banged so against the door that she had to take it out of there. She threw it in the fire, but of course it would not burn. However hard she tried, there seemed no way to be rid of the stick.

Finally, from the back of her closet she fetched the tattered bundle of old clothes she had once worn, wound around the old axe. She hid the stick among them along with the cap and instantly all was still.

That night the husband demanded the wishing stick that he might call forth their food. But the old woman sighed and said it was lost and nowhere to be found.

"Fool!" roared the husband, and up he rose and began to search for it.

Outside there grew a rumble of thunder in the sky, and the wind lashed the trees against the castle wall. It became dark so quickly that they lit candles to see by. And still he searched, both high and low, in every nook and cranny, even to the shadows that lurked at the back of the woman's closet, though he did not touch the filthy ball of rags he found there. At last, exhausted, he lay down to sleep.

And the woman lay long and still by his side, listening to the wind whistling around the walls, until by and by, the man began to snore.

Then quietly she crept from beneath the covers and stole across the room to her closet. And she stripped off her fine clothes and fetched the old rags wound round the axe and put them on.

And all the while the old man lay with wide eyes watching her, for he had suspected her of hiding the stick and had but pretended to be asleep.

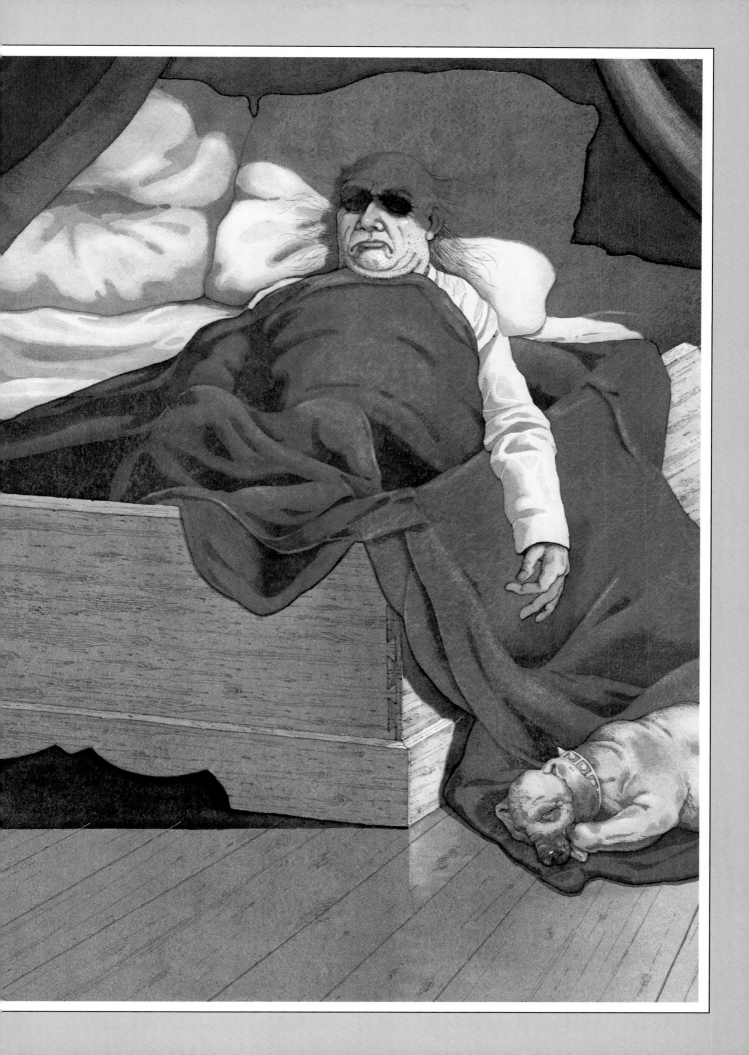

Then taking up the cap and stick
the old woman hurried from the
castle and was soon over the wall and
into the wood. Oh, what a feeling of
freedom came over her then, and she
wanted nothing more than to be
happily gathering wood there as she
once had. But close behind her came
the old man with the axe.

Slowly she felt her way through the
murky wood lit now and then by
distant lightning, and at last she
stood at the base of the tree felled by
the bolt. She called down into the
hole and up leapt the little man with
the long grey beard.

"Well," he said when he saw her
standing there. "If it isn't the woman
who freed me from the tree. Dreadful
night, isn't it? And how have the cap
and stick served you? Well, I trust."

"No, not well at all," she said, and
told how things had gone from bad to
worse with her, and how her husband
had daily grown more cruel and had
at last decided to be done with her.
And she said she more than half
wished that none of it had happened
and that she was simply left to gather
her wood in the forest as before.

"Well, that's easily enough arranged," he said. "You need but give back the gifts and all will be as before."

"By all means, take them then," she said as she handed him the cap and stick.

But suddenly there was a shriek from behind a nearby tree and out burst the husband. "No!" he bellowed, and ran at them with the axe raised above his head.

What happened next was hidden from sight, for at that moment a blinding bolt of lightning struck the forest where they stood. And when the woman could see again, her husband was gone, and the tree stood whole. And the little man stood before it with the stick in his hand.

He turned and smiled. Then twining his long beard twice about his neck, he pressed the crushed cap on his head, winked once, and was gone.

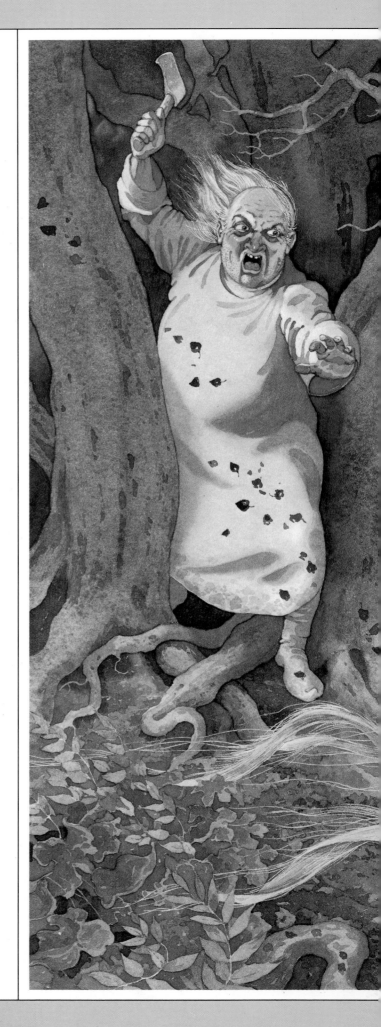

From that day forward the woman gathered wood in the forest as she had before. Still, there was one old tree that she did not go near, where more than the wind moaned in the branches.

And though she was not wealthy, she was well and lived at peace in her small bark shack tucked secretly among the trees. And for all I know, she lives there still.